To Jenni, my ray of sunshine on many a cloudy day. To my parents, Tom and Barbara, and brother, Brian, for always believing that, someday, I could "make it rain." And to Liam, who I know was born to make this world a better place.

Cody the Cloud

PRT0415C

Printed in the United States
Library of Congress Control Number: 2014920123
ISBN-13: 978-1-63177-001-2

www.mascotbooks.com

CODY the CLOUD

Written by
Kevin Mulhern

Illustrated by
Dodot Asmoro

Among a big, white fluffy crowd
Lived the tiny Cody the Cloud.
Above the earth way up high,
He floated across the big blue sky.

Cody floated everywhere,
Through weather stormy, bright, and fair.
Always moving, he never stopped,
Over oceans and high mountaintops.

But though he floated high and free,
Cody never felt happy.
What was it that caused him so much pain?
Cody the Cloud could not make it rain.

He was too small, his shape too slim,
The other clouds made fun of him.
"You're too different, you're too small,
And you can't make it rain at all."

Only in Cody's magnificent dreams
Did he fill up the lakes, the rivers, and streams.
But no matter how hard Cody tried,
He could never make it rain outside.

Years passed and Cody still hadn't grown,
And he wanted to be left alone.
So he drifted off without a sound
And floated gently to the ground.

Cody landed and was shocked to see
A small boy sitting in a large tree.
The boy asked Cody with a questioning stare,
"What are you doing way down here?"

Cody moved closer and told him why.
"I don't belong up in the sky.
I'm not special, I'm very plain.
What kind of cloud can't make it rain?"

The boy looked closely at Cody the Cloud
And after a moment, he said aloud,
"I also feel like I don't belong.
I'm small too, and not very strong.

I have short legs and small, bony arms
And I can't work on my father's farm.
So I just sit here in this tree
Because the other boys make fun of me."

Cody told the boy, "That's just not fair.
But you and I make quite the pair."
So they talked while the sun shined bright.
They talked and talked until it was night.

Time passed and by summer's end,
Cody and the boy became best friends.
Each night they lay beneath the stars
And said, "I like you the way you are."

But each afternoon after the fields were plowed,
The kids picked on the boy and Cody the Cloud.
Other clouds joined in on the fun.
They pointed and laughed until the day was done.

Still, Cody and the boy stood by each other.
They weren't just friends, they were close like brothers.
Sitting together by that great big tree
Was the only place they wanted to be.

But no rain fell and the earth was dry,
And one day the boy began to cry,
"Our crops won't grow and the well is empty.
There's no food to eat, and we're all thirsty!"

Cody looked up at the blazing sun.
"Yes, it's much too hot for everyone.
Your farm needs rain, that's certainly true.
I just wish there was something I could do."

The boy sat quietly in the heat,
Then suddenly, leaped up to
his feet.
"Cody, you can fly into the sky!
And make it rain, please,
please try!"

Cody looked away and bowed his head.
"I think I'll go to bed instead.
I'd much rather lay here and mope.
I can't make it rain, there is no hope."

The boy said, "I know we may feel small.
We may not be strong, we may not be tall.
But you and I can change the weather.
Side-by-side, we'll do it together."

And although Cody the Cloud said, "No,"
The boy climbed on his back and said, "Let's go!"
So up into the air they climbed
While the birds chirped and the sun shined.

Cody tried and tried, but he soon quit.
"I can't do this, I give up, that's it!"
Down toward the ground Cody flew,
Then the boy whispered, "I believe in you."

Then up into the sky, Cody soared.
He'd never heard those words before.
The boy said, "Cody, just try again.
You can do it, you're my best friend."

Cody's eyes filled with tears of joy
Thanks to the words of that small boy.
Down to the earth Cody's tears fell,
Onto the fields and into the wells.

And so this small, unlikely team
Filled up the lakes, the rivers, and streams.
Flowers purple, yellow, and pink
Blossomed because they had water to drink.

Down on the ground life sprung anew.
The plants turned greener while the crops grew.
There was water for the cattle, pigs, and lambs.
The children all shouted and laughed as they swam.

The farmers looked up as they felt the raindrops.
"It's not too late to save our summer crops.
The rain is falling, the heat's gone away.
Cody and the boy have saved the day!"

Cody and the boy landed back on the ground.
The other boys and clouds gathered 'round.
"You may both be small, that may be true,
But we were wrong to make fun of you."

Cody the Cloud and the boy both smiled
And saw far away, across many miles,
A small rainbow appearing in the sky
So beautiful that everyone cried.

And Cody the Cloud knew what it all meant:
You don't have to be big to be important.

the

End

Kevin Mulhern has enjoyed a career writing for television, radio, newspapers, and magazines, and was guided early in his career by his dearly missed, beloved mentor and friend, the comedic actor/writer, Phil Hartman. Kevin is currently a radio producer and on-air talent at 94 WHJY in Providence, Rhode Island. He lives with his wife Jennifer, son Liam, and dog Kreugas in Rhode Island. *Cody the Cloud* is his first children's book.

Cody the Cloud can be purchased at www.CodyTheCloud.com, where you can also find information on "Cody" news, events, reviews, and contact the author, Kevin Mulhern. Also, "like" the official *Cody the Cloud* Facebook page at www.facebook.com/CodyTheCloud.

Have a book idea?

Contact us at:

Mascot Books
560 Herndon Parkway
Suite 120
Herndon, VA 20170

info@mascotbooks.com | www.mascotbooks.com